Becky the Brave

~ A STORY ABOUT EPILEPSY ~

WRITTEN BY **Laurie Lears**

ILLUSTRATED BY **Gail Piazza**

Albert Whitman & Company
Morton Grove, Illinois

For Maura. — L. L.

To my mother, Hope. — G. P.
And with special thanks to Alyson and Elizabeth.

Library of Congress Cataloging-in-Publication Data
Lears, Laurie.
Becky the brave: a story about epilepsy / by Laurie Lears; illustrated by Gail Piazza.
p. cm.
Summary: Nothing seems to scare Sarah's big sister Becky, until having an epileptic seizure
makes her reluctant to return to school, and so Sarah summons her own courage
to explain the disease to the other students.
ISBN 0-8075-0601-X (hardcover)
[1. Epilepsy — Fiction.   2. Courage — Fiction.   3. Sisters — Fiction.
4. Schools — Fiction.]   I. Piazza, Gail, ill. II. Title.
PZ7.L46365 Bd 2002   [E] — dc21   2001004094

The art is rendered in pastel on Canson pastel paper.
The design is by Scott Piehl.

For more information about Albert Whitman & Company,
please visit our web site at www.albertwhitman.com.

EXTENSION

~ Note ~

About three hundred thousand American children have epilepsy. Usually, there's no known cause. The symptoms of epilepsy are seizures resulting from disruptions in the brain's electrical system. Seizures may affect a child's consciousness, movement, or behavior. If the whole brain is affected, the child may drop suddenly to the floor, or have a convulsion where she falls, stiffens, shakes, and slowly regains consciousness. Or she may stare blankly for a few seconds, or her muscles may suddenly jerk. These are all known as generalized seizures.

If only part of the brain is involved, the result is a partial seizure: uncontrolled shaking of an arm or leg, unusual feelings of nausea or pain, changes in mood or sensation, or the sense of a distorted environment, where things look and sound different from what they really are. Some children have partial seizures that suspend awareness and cause automatic movements like chewing, plucking at clothes, mumbling, and in some cases, wandering or running in apparent fear.

First aid keeps the child safe until the seizure is over. If he is having a convulsion, place something soft and flat under the child's head, loosen clothing that can obstruct breathing, and roll him gently onto one side to prevent choking. Nothing should be placed in the mouth, and no restraint should be applied. Most seizures end after a minute or two; awareness slowly returns. At this point, the child needs reassurance and support. If another seizure begins soon after the first, or a single seizure lasts more than five minutes, call an ambulance.

Childhood epilepsy is treated with seizure-preventing medication. If seizures persist, other treatments, like surgery, brain stimulation, or diet may be tried. Some children become seizure-free on medication, and with a doctor's supervision, may be tapered off the meds after a couple of years. Other children continue to have some seizures despite treatment. Some have severe epilepsy that does not yield to treatment.

Because of the nature and unpredictability of seizures, the negative reactions of others, and some side effects of treatment, epilepsy is tough on children, parents, and siblings. Studies show the best adjustment comes when parents are open and can talk about the condition with teachers and others without embarrassment and help their children to do the same.

All kids with epilepsy want one thing: to be just normal kids and to be treated like everyone else. That's not always easy to achieve, but openness, courage, and information can make a big difference, as this story shows.

Ann Scherer
Senior Director, Communications
Epilepsy Foundation

For further information about epilepsy, visit the Epilepsy Foundation's web site at www.epilepsyfoundation.org or call toll free at 1-800-332-1000.

Becky is my big sister. In many ways we are alike, but there is one big difference between us. Becky is brave . . . and I am not.

On the first day at our new school, I am so nervous my legs turn to stone. But Becky holds my hand and says, "Come on, Sarah, I'll take you to your classroom." And somehow my legs begin to move.

After school Becky and I walk home together. As we pass a fenced yard, a big dog charges through the gate toward us. I step backward and scream.

But Becky crosses her arms in front of her and says, "NO!" And that dog stops right in his tracks and scoots back to his house.

Becky is even brave about having epilepsy. She takes medicine so she won't have seizures. But sometimes the medicine doesn't work. One evening while we're setting the table for dinner, Becky suddenly gets stiff and falls to the floor. Her face turns bluish and a gurgling sound comes from her throat.

I push the chair away so Becky won't hurt herself.

"Mom, Dad! Come quick!" I shout. "Becky is having a seizure!"

Dad gently rolls Becky to her side and Mom slips a flat pillow under her head. Becky's arms and legs begin to jerk. The jerking seems to go on forever. But at last the seizure stops and Becky sighs.

I let out my breath, too. Even though I know the seizure doesn't hurt Becky, it frightens me more than most anything. I kneel beside Becky and rub her arm until she wakes up. At last she looks at me sleepily. "Don't worry, Sarah. I'm okay," she says slowly.

Mom takes Becky to the doctor to see if her medicine needs to be changed. The doctor gives Becky new pills to try. But she can't promise that her seizures will go away for good.

Becky is quiet when she gets home. "What's wrong?" I ask.

Becky's eyes fill with tears. "I'm afraid I might have a seizure at
school," she says. "Mom told the teacher and the nurse, but
I don't want my new friends to know I have epilepsy."

I can hardly believe my ears! I didn't think Becky was afraid of
anything!

From then on, when Becky drops me off at my classroom,
I squeeze her hand and make a wish that she won't have a seizure
at school.

But one day, just as school lets out, Mom comes to my classroom
instead of Becky. "Becky had a seizure," Mom tells me. "She's waiting
in the car."

"Oh, no!" I cry, and I rush outside to see Becky. She is huddled in the back seat of the car looking tired and sad.

When we get home Becky heads straight to our bedroom and closes the door. She won't even come out for dinner.

At bedtime, I hear Becky sniffling and know she's been crying. "Mom packed your favorite cookies for lunch tomorrow," I say, trying to cheer her up.

"I'm not going back to school," Becky tells me. "After I had my seizure everyone stared at me, and some kids even laughed!"

"That wasn't nice," I say. "But you have to go to school." And my stomach does a somersault just thinking about going to school without her.

"Well, I'm not going!" says Becky, and she rolls over and pulls the blanket over her head. I lie awake and worry for a long time.

The next morning Becky tells Mom she doesn't feel well. Mom takes Becky's temperature and peers down her throat. "You look fine," she says. But Becky shakes her head and climbs back into bed.

"I guess you'll have to walk by yourself today," Mom tells me.
"I don't want to go alone," I say, though no one seems to listen.
I glare at Becky and stomp out the door. I'm so angry I almost
forget to be afraid.

But when I get to school, my knees begin to wobble. I shuffle down the long hallway and miss feeling Becky's warm hand around mine. As I pass Becky's classroom, I take a quick peek inside. All the kids are at their desks, and I notice Becky's empty seat.

"Hey! Aren't you Becky's sister?" a boy calls. "Is Becky still in the hospital?"

I blink in surprise. "Becky's not at the hospital," I say.

"Is Becky going to get better?" asks a girl in a pink shirt.

My heart begins to pound and I want to disappear. But I realize Becky's classmates don't know anything about epilepsy. Maybe I can help them understand why she had a seizure.

I step into the room and look at Becky's teacher. Mr. Hopkins
smiles at me. "I was just about to tell the class about Becky," he says.
"But you go ahead, Sarah."

I take a deep breath. "Becky is not sick; she has epilepsy," I say.
"Her brain sometimes gives off too much electricity all at once,
and that makes her have a seizure."

"Are her seizures dangerous?" asks a boy in the front row.

I shake my head. "Becky could hurt herself when she falls," I say. "But the seizure doesn't hurt her. Even though it looks scary, the seizure goes away by itself, and Becky's just tired afterwards."

"Why didn't Becky tell us she had seizures?" asks the boy.

I shrug. "Epilepsy is only a little part of Becky. She can run fast and play the trumpet and she's good with animals. Maybe she was afraid you wouldn't get to know the rest of her if you found out about her seizures."

Becky's friends nod as if they understand, and Mr. Hopkins thanks me for coming. I back out the door and hurry to my classroom.

The day seems to drag on forever. In the afternoon, the girl in the pink shirt brings me Becky's homework folder.

Finally the dismissal bell rings, and I dash outside. I run all the way to our house without stopping. I can't wait to tell Becky about my day!

Becky is still in her pajamas when I get home. "Guess what!" I say. "I visited your classroom today!"

But Becky doesn't seem to care. She barely looks at me as I place her folder on the couch. "Here's your homework," I say softly.

Becky frowns. "I told you I'm not going back to school," she says, pushing the folder away.

Suddenly a stack of papers slides out of the folder and scatters on the floor. As Becky gathers the papers together, her eyes light up and a smile creeps across her face. "Look!" she cries, handing me one of the papers.

I read the note she gives me:

Dear Becky,
We miss you! Your sister told us about epilepsy. Now we understand it better. Please hurry back to school!
Your friend,
Courtney

Becky reads all the notes from her classmates and then reaches out to hug me. "Thank you for talking to my friends," she says. "How did you get so brave, Sarah?"

"I learned it from you!" I say. And I hug my sister right back!